Dear Lefy
Have fun
reading this
book and
have a happy
Hanuka
Love
auntie
&
uncle

Published in the United States by Random House Children's Books,
a division of Random House, Inc., New York, New York 10019.
The Apprentice and logo are trademarks of
JMBP, Inc.
www.randomhouse.com/kids
Educators and librarians, for a variety of teaching tools, visit us at
www.randomhouse.com/teachers
ISBN 0-375-83719-1
Printed in the United States of America
First Edition   10 9 8 7 6 5 4 3 2 1

JACK
and the
BEANSTALK

A fairy tale adapted by
Primarius Corporation

Illustrations by
Paul Meisel

Do you know the real story of Jack and the beanstalk?
Well, my name is Jack. I live in a house by the sea,
and I have a secret to share with you.

I like riding my red bicycle on the beach.
One day, I met a man who looked very sad.

"Why are you sad?" I asked.

"I never had a shiny red bike," the man said,
"but I'll trade you my magic beans for your bike."

"They're magic?" I asked.

"If you plant them, they will take you on
a great adventure," the man said.

"**WOW!** That sounds cool!"

So I traded my bicycle for the special beans.

"You traded your new bicycle for magic beans?"
my mom asked. "There's no such thing as magic."

I planted them anyway,
just in case.

The ground began
to shake and rumble.
I couldn't believe it.
The magic beans
were growing right
before my eyes!

A beanstalk burst
out of the ground and
headed straight into the sea.
I hopped on for the ride of my life.

Deeper and deeper into the ocean I dove.
At the bottom, I found a treasure chest full
of gold. I took a few of the sparkling coins.

Suddenly an octopus called out
from the shadows.

"I'm Oscar the Octopus.
I rule this sea.
You have to ask
before taking from me."

"I'm sorry, Oscar. I just wanted a few gold coins."

"That's okay," Oscar said. "Next time just ask before you take."

"Thanks!" I jumped back on the beanstalk
and shot out of the water.

Oscar waved goodbye as I rode up into the mountains.

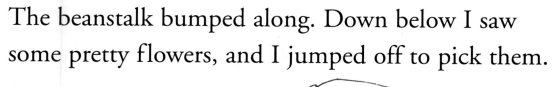

The beanstalk bumped along. Down below I saw
some pretty flowers, and I jumped off to pick them.

Suddenly I heard a booming voice.

"I'm Gerald the Giant!
FE-FI-FO-FUM!
You have to ask
before you take some!"

"Sorry, Gerald. I learned from Oscar the Octopus to ask before I take. I didn't know these flowers were yours!"

"That's okay," the giant said. "You can take them with you."

I sped back to the beanstalk and hopped on.
I soared high into the sky. **Whoosh!**

On top of a cloud I saw a big castle.
It looked like it was made out of chocolate!
I couldn't believe my eyes.

An entire castle made out of chocolate?
Could it be true?

Down swooped a large hawk.
"I'm Harriet the Hawk,"
she squawked from a cloud.
*"Taking without asking
is never allowed."*

"May I please have a piece of your chocolate castle?"

"Why, yes," the hawk said, "and thank you for asking!" I hopped back on the beanstalk and was ready to go home!

My mother looked really worried when I got home.
"Where have you been?" she asked.

"I have been on a magical adventure, and I brought you some presents— gold coins from the sea, flowers from the mountains, and chocolate from a castle in the sky!"

My mom was so happy with the gifts.
Most of all she was glad to have me
back home, safe and sound.

So that's the real story,
you've heard it from me.
Never take without asking
and always say please!